PROJECTS ABOUT
Nineteenth-Century Chinese Immigrants

Marian Broida

Marshall Cavendish
Benchmark
New York

Acknowledgments

The author wishes to thank Suellen Cheng, curator, and Sheryl Nakano, collections assistant, El Pueblo Historical Monument, Chinese American Museum, Los Angeles; Robert Fisher, collections manager, Wing Luke Asian Museum, Seattle; Valery Garrett; David Kleit, PhD; and Shuh Yun Liu.
And thanks to the following for their help in testing activities: Shaina and Rachel Andres, Carolyn Cohen, Beatrice Misher.

Marshall Cavendish Benchmark
99 White Plains Road
Tarrytown, NY 10591-9001
www.marshallcavendish.us

Library of Congress Cataloging-in-Publication Data
Broida, Marian.
        Projects about nineteenth-century Chinese Immigrants / by Marian Broida.
        p. cm. — (Hands-on history)
Includes bibliographical references and index.
Summary: Includes social studies projects taken from Chinese immigrants
of the 19th century.
        ISBN 0-7614-1978-0
1. Chinese Americans—History—Study and teaching—Activity
programs—Juvenile literature. 2. Immigrants—United States—
History—Study and teaching—Activity programs—Juvenile literature.
3. Chinese Americans—Social life and customs—Study and teaching—Activity
programs—Juvenile literature. I. Title. II. Series.
CURR E184.C5B73 2005 2006
973'.04951—dc22
        2004027458

Map and illustrations by Rodica Prato
Photo research by Joan Meisel
Photo credits: Courtesy Central Pacific Railroad Photographic History Museum, ©2005, CPRR.org, 22 (right). *Corbis:* Bettmann, 22 (left), 23 (top); Charles & Josette Lenars, 28. *Getty Images:* Hulton Archive, 8; MPI, 20; AFP, 36. *North Wind Picture Archives:* 1, 4, 7, 34. *Online Archive of California,* BANC PIC 1999.073:01-PIC., 39. *Photo Researchers, Inc.:* Ken Lax, 17; Omikron, 23 (bottom).

Contents

Shops in the Chinese section of San Francisco in about 1870.

1
Introduction

This is a book about people who came from China to the United States during the 1800s (the **nineteenth century**). Most were young men who wanted to earn money for their families in China. They mined for gold, laid **railroad ties**, started businesses, farmed, and fished. Most didn't plan to stay more than a few years. But many did stay, becoming **immigrants**.

Life for the Chinese in America was hard. Though some Americans welcomed them, the Chinese faced much **discrimination**.

Chinese **culture** is thousands of years old, rich in art and learning. The Chinese who came to America brought their own ways of writing, building, cooking, eating, and celebrating.

In this book, you'll learn about the lives of these hardworking and sometimes very lonely people. You'll build a gold miner's scale, practice some **calligraphy,** make an **abacus** and a fan, and paint your face like a Chinese actor's.

Enjoy your travels to the past. As Chinese immigrants might say, *Lui sing yu fai*—Happy journey!

This map shows the part of China called Guangdong Province, the first home of most nineteenth-century Chinese immigrants. Many people in this part of China suffered from hunger and war during the 1800s. Men from Guangdong came to America to help their families in China.

Chinese immigrants aboard a steamship on their way to San Francisco. Tales in China said lumps of gold could be picked up off the ground in California. Early Chinese immigrants called California "Gold Mountain."

Chinese workers panning for gold in California.

2
The 1850s

Before 1849 very few Chinese lived in America. But in that year something happened in California that brought travelers from around the world: gold was discovered. Tens of thousands of Chinese men boarded ships to San Francisco to mine for gold. Very few got rich, but most earned more than they had in China.

When gold got harder to find, some Chinese returned to China or moved elsewhere in America. Most stayed out west, often living in big cities in communities called **Chinatown**.

Few Chinese women or children lived in the United States in the 1850s. A small number, mostly families of merchants, joined their husbands and fathers. Often, young men left their wives and children alone in China for years or forever, sending money to support them. The United States government did not allow most Chinese men to marry American women. Many Chinese immigrants lived as **bachelors** all their lives.

Gold Miner's Scale and Gold Nuggets

You are a Chinese man. Two months ago you took over a mine on a riverbank from earlier miners who moved away. You work carefully, shoveling sand into your **rocker**. You find a lot of gold dust and **nuggets** that the first miners missed. You don't talk about your success, for fear other miners will steal your spot.

You take some gold dust to the store to buy food. The white store-keeper weighs it. "What do you want to buy? " he asks.
"Chicken and pork," you say.

"Must be doing all right," says the storekeeper. "Otherwise you'd buy just rice."

Gold Miner's Scale
You will need:

- scissors
- 2 solid-colored disposable cups, paper or plastic
- a 1-hole punch
- embroidery thread, about 6 feet long
- 2 beads, each about ½ inch around, with large holes (Pony beads)
- wire coat hanger
- a few screws, nuts, nails, or small stones

1. Cut the upper parts off the two cups, leaving the cups about 1 to 1½ inches tall. Make both cups the same height.

2. Punch three holes near the top of each cup, evenly spaced around the rim.

3. Cut six pieces of embroidery thread, each 10 to 12 inches long.

4. Push one piece of thread through one of the holes in a cup and make a knot near the end of the thread. If you have trouble, ask an adult for help. Repeat with all the other holes.

5. Gather the three threads tied to one cup and push the free ends through a bead. Tie these three ends together around one end of the solid bar of the hanger. Ask for help if you need it.

6. Repeat with the other cup at the other end of the hanger.

7. Hang the scale on a doorknob. If one cup hangs lower than the other, move the low cup closer to the middle of the hanger until the scale hangs evenly.

8. Make "gold" nuggets (explained next) and pour some into one cup. In the other cup, place a screw, nut, small stone, or another heavy object. Add and subtract objects or gold nuggets until the cups hang evenly.

Gold Nuggets or Dust
You will need:

- newspaper
- disposable rubber gloves
- handful of sand

- 1-2 tablespoons gold-colored acrylic or tempera paint
- dinner-sized paper plate

Spread the newspaper on your work surface and put on the gloves. Pour the sand and paint onto the plate. Mix them thoroughly with your hands. Spread the painted sand on the plate and allow to dry. The larger clumps will look like gold nuggets, the single grains like gold dust.

Chinese Rice and Green Beans

You are a young man, seventeen years old. After months aboard a crowded ship, you finally arrive at *Dai Fow,* or Big City, the Chinese name for San Francisco. The trip lasted longer than you expected because of bad weather. You ran out of the food you brought before the voyage ended. For days you have eaten only a little boiled rice.

As you leave the ship, carrying all your belongings in a straw basket on a stick, you hear a voice in Chinese calling out the name of the part of China you are from. The man says he will guide you and other passengers to a building where you can stay until you are settled. You follow him through the city, gazing about you at the people and buildings you pass. But mainly, as you walk, you think about your empty belly.

When you arrive, you are served a meal of rice, Chinese vegetables, and meat. You make yourself eat slowly, even though you want to gobble it all at once.

Chinese-Style Boiled Rice
You will need:

- 1 cup long-grain white rice (not instant)
- large, heavy saucepan (at least 3-quart size) with tight-fitting lid
- water
- liquid measuring cup

- very fine strainer
- stove
- large spoon
- timer
- pot holder
- trivet (a stand for hot pots)

- forks or chopsticks
- serving bowls
- 1 teaspoon soy sauce per serving, or 1 portion Chinese-style green beans (recipe follows)

1. Ask an adult to help. Wash your hands.

2. Put the rice in the pot. To clean the rice, add enough cold water to cover the rice. Stir. Pour through the strainer. Do this three or four times.

3. Put cleaned rice back into the saucepan.

4. Carefully measure 1½ cups of cold water. Pour it onto the rice.

5. Place the pot on the stove and stir the rice and water once.
   Turn the heat to medium. Leave the pot uncovered. Watch carefully for "rice eyes" (pits in the surface of the rice). When you see them (or after about three minutes, even if you can't), turn the heat very low and cover the pot.

6. Set the timer for twenty minutes. Important: do not remove the pot lid!

7. When the timer sounds, use the pot holder to take the pot off the stove and place it on the trivet without removing the lid. Let the pot sit, covered, another ten to fifteen minutes.

8. Take off the lid and fluff the rice with a fork or chopsticks.

9. Spoon the rice into individual serving bowls. To eat, lift the bowl toward your chin and scoop the rice into your mouth. Use chopsticks if you know how.

10. This recipe serves at least three people.

Chinese-Style Green Beans
You will need:

- about 2 cups of green beans (fresh or frozen)
- colander
- sharp knife
- cutting board
- 2 scallions
- 1 cup water or chicken broth
- 2 tablespoons soy sauce
- ¼ teaspoon powdered ginger, optional
- ½ teaspoon crushed garlic, optional
- ¾ cup walnut or almond pieces
- 2 tablespoons toasted sesame oil or any vegetable oil
- metal tablespoon
- small bowl
- measuring spoons
- large frying pan or wok (Chinese frying pan) with lid
- stove
- spatula or wooden spoon
- pot holder
- fork

1. Have an adult help. Wash your hands.

2. If you are using fresh beans, rinse them in the colander. Cut off their ends on the cutting board. Discard the ends. Cut the beans into 1- to 2-inch pieces. Put them back in the colander.

3. Rinse the scallions. On the cutting board, trim off the white hairy parts and throw them away. Slice the rest of the scallions, white and green parts, into small sections about ¼ inch long. Add to the beans.

4. Pour the water or broth into the measuring cup. Add the soy sauce, ginger, and garlic to the cup. Stir carefully with the tablespoon.

5. Pour the nuts into the small bowl.

6. With the measuring spoons, measure the oil and pour it into the pan. Tilt the pan so the oil coats the inside, and set the pan on the stove.

7. Turn the heat to high.

8. Count 30 seconds, then add the beans and scallions to the pan. Stir with the spatula or wooden spoon, using the pot holder to hold the pan. Stir in the nuts, if using, coating them with oil. Cook, stirring constantly, about two minutes.

9. Carefully stir in the water mixture. Cook about five to ten minutes, stirring often. Now and then, poke a bean with a fork to see if it is tender.

10. When the beans are tender but still a little crunchy, turn off the stove. Using the pot holder and wooden spoon or spatula, spoon portions over the rice you made before. This recipe serves three people.

Chinese Calligraphy

You are a twenty-year-old gold miner. Ever since you arrived in America, you have sent money home each month. But yesterday other miners stole your gold dust. Now you have no money to send.

Sadly, you mix dry ink with water, dip in your brush, and draw Chinese **characters** on paper. "Next month I will have better luck," you write in Chinese.

You end the letter as usual, "I send blessings that everything is peaceful," and sign your name.

A Chinese man teaches his grandson the art of calligraphy.

You will need:

- newspaper
- medium-sized paintbrush (A Chinese calligraphy brush or another round-tipped brush is best.)
- jar of washable black ink
- several sheets of solid-color construction paper
- jar of water
- paper towels for spills

1. Spread newspaper on your work surface.

2. Dip the brush into the ink and wipe the extra ink off on the rim of the jar.

3. Sit up straight. Hold the brush straight up and down. Copy the first character at right onto the paper, making the lines in the order shown below.

4. Copy the second character below the first. (The Chinese usually write from the top to the bottom of a page.)

5. When you are done, carefully rinse your brush and let it dry before putting it away.

The Chinese do not use an alphabet. Instead, they write characters standing for whole words or ideas. These two characters together mean peaceful. The first by itself, means flat, or nothing happening. The second shows a woman under the roof of a house. The Chinese believe that a woman makes a house peaceful.

In the 1870s prejudiced Americans held rallies against the Chinese.

3

The 1860s and 1870s

In 1865 an American railroad company hired a few Chinese men to help build the Central Pacific Railroad, the western part of the **transcontinental** railroad, which went from Sacramento, California, to Omaha, Nebraska. Few Americans wanted the job, so the company advertised in China. Thousands of Chinese workers came to hammer steel rails into place and to blast a way through the mountains. The work was hard and dangerous, but the Chinese labored with skill and courage.

Chinese immigrants worked long hours at other jobs as well: washing clothes in laundries, making shoes in factories, or working in businesses like groceries that served other Chinese.

Hard as the Chinese worked, **prejudice** against them grew. Some Americans who once welcomed the immigrants now said they ought to leave. These Americans feared the Chinese would take too many jobs. They were also suspicious of Chinese ways.

The Transcontinental Railroad

There were not enough workers in America willing to take on the hard work of building the first railroad to connect the east coast to the west. The Central Pacific Railroad company advertised for workers in China. Charles Crocker organized the project and said this of the Chinese workers: "Wherever we put them, we found them good . . . and they worked themselves into our favor to such an extent that if we found we were in a hurry for a job of work, it was better to put Chinese on at once."

Over twelve thousand Chinese men came to America to help build the Central Pacific Railroad. Chinese workers were only paid about $30 a month.

A Chinese workers' camp in Nevada. Each group of workers, called gangs, had their own cook who prepared meals, including meat from live pigs and chickens that they kept for special weekend meals.

The Secret Town trestle had to be buried during the building of the Central Pacific Railroad. Chinese workers buried it and filled the valley in with dirt from the mountainside.

Fan

You are posing with your parents for a photograph—the first you can remember. Your father, a **merchant,** wears his best silk robes and a black satin cap. Your mother has **bound feet**. Her tiny shoes peep from beneath her most elegant skirt. You wear your best silk jacket and trousers and hold a folding fan.

Suddenly you hear a chirp from your pet cricket across the room. You can't help smiling.

"Look serious!" scolds your mother. "He's about to take the picture!"

You will need:

- 1 sheet solid-color construction paper, about 8½ by 11 inches
- dinner plate
- pencil
- cup, can, or glass
- scissors
- colored markers
- poster board, about 6 inches on each side
- ruler
- a 1-hole punch
- ribbon, yarn, embroidery thread, or gold gift thread (5-6 inches long)
- double-sided tape

1. Lay the construction paper so the longer side is nearest you. Lay the upper half of the plate on top of the paper, as shown. Trace around the plate with the pencil.

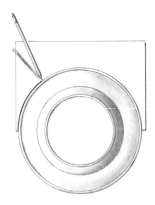

2. Lay the upper half of the cup or glass on top of the paper, as shown. Trace around it.

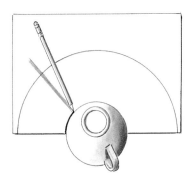

3. Cut along the two lines you drew. Keep only the middle part of the paper for your fan.

4. With the markers, make a design on the fan, on one side only. Set the fan aside.

5. Lay the ruler along the bottom edge of the poster board so the corner of the poster board lines up with the left edge of the ruler. Every ¾ of an inch make a dot on the bottom edge of the paper until you have made eight dots. (Have an adult help.) Do the same along the top edge. Your dots should line up. Using the ruler to keep your lines straight, draw a line between each pair of dots (one on the bottom and one at the top). Cut along these lines. You should have seven strips.

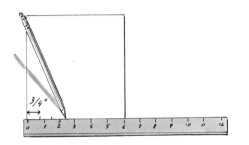

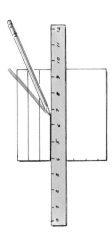

6. Punch a hole near the short bottom edge of one strip and lay it on top of the next, so the edges match. Put your pencil point through the hole you punched and mark a spot on the second strip. Punch a hole in that spot. Repeat until you have punched all the strips.

7. Stack the strips so all the holes line up. Run a piece of ribbon through the holes, tie the ribbon, and trim off the ribbon ends neatly.

8. Number the strips, in order, writing lightly in pencil. The top strip is number 1, the next is number 2, and so on.

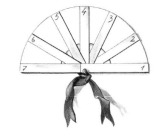

9. Lay your fan picture-side down. Place a strip of double-sided tape along the straight bottom edge to the middle. Lay strip number 1 on top of the tape.

10. Use double-sided tape to stick strip number 7 in the same way to the fan's bottom left corner, along the straight bottom edge, and to the middle of the bottom edge.

11. Lay a strip of double-sided tape from the center of the bottom edge, pointing away from you, to the middle of the top edge. Attach strip number 4. Arrange the other strips evenly, in order, across the back of the fan. Tape each in place the same way.

12. With the fan still upside down, gently fold strip number 1 until it is directly over strip number 2. The paper will come with the strip. Press strip number 1 down. You will make a crease in the fan.

13. Now pick up strips number 1 and number 2 together, and lay them on top of strip number 3. Again, press down firmly, making a crease.

14. Repeat until all the strips are stacked, and there are creases between all the strips.

15. Now try opening and closing your fan.

Chinese students use abacuses at a school in Nankin, China.

Abacus

You are sitting in your father's Chinese grocery. He is adding up prices on his abacus, a wooden frame with beads on rods. When the customers leave, he lays it in your lap.

"I'll show you how to use it," he says. "See this crossbar? The beads above it are called heaven. The beads below it are called earth. A bead in heaven is worth five earth beads on the same rod."

He pushes all the beads on all the rods away from the crossbar. "This is how you start. To count a bead, you push it toward the crossbar."

You slide an earth bead up to the crossbar, on the far-right rod.

"You just counted 'one'," says your father.

You will need:

- 7 bamboo or wooden skewers (thin rods), at least 1 inch longer than longest side of the meat tray
- 1 piece of fine sandpaper
- ruler
- cardboard or Styrofoam food tray, about 6 by 8 inches, preferably black, cleaned and dried
- about 50 Pony beads (plastic beads, about ¼ inch long, available in craft stores) or other beads with large holes

1. Blunt the skewer tips a bit by rubbing them on the sandpaper.

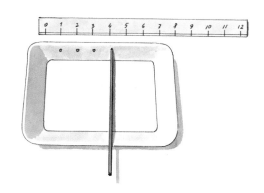

2. Place the plastic tray face up as shown. Lay the ruler just above it.

3. Using the tip of a skewer, poke six dents or small holes about 1 inch apart, on the far, long upright wall of the tray. Your marks should be on the vertical (up-and-down) inner side of the tray, not on its flat bottom, in as straight a line as possible.

4. Poke a skewer through the first dent or hole. Slide seven beads onto the end of the skewer nearest you. Now poke the skewer's near end through the wall of the meat tray that is closest to you. Try not to make your holes bigger than you need to.

5. Repeat step 4 with five more skewers, leaving one unused.

6. On each of the skewers, move two beads away from you and five beads toward you.

7. The last skewer is your crossbar. Poke one end through one of the tray's short walls, about a third of the way down.

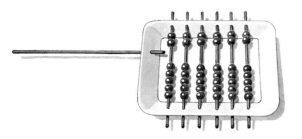

8. Slide the crossbar across the tray, over or under the other skewers. The crossbar should come close enough to the other skewers to keep the beads on the correct side: two beads above and five below. If some of your skewers are crooked, this might mean you have to push the crossbar over some skewers and under others.

9. When the crossbar has passed all the other skewers, poke it through the opposite wall of the tray.

To show a number on an abacus:

1. Lay the abacus flat. Push all beads away from the crossbar.

2. To show the number 4, use the rod farthest to the right.
Push four earth beads toward the crossbar.

3. You can show the number 5 two ways. On the far-right rod, you can push all five earth beads toward the crossbar. Or, on this same rod, you can push one heaven bead toward the crossbar, with all the earth beads pushed away. Each heaven bead on this rod is worth 5.

4. On the rod that is second from the right, each earth bead is worth 10 and each heaven bead is worth 50.

5. On the third rod from the right, each earth bead is worth 100, and each heaven bead worth 500.

6. To show the number 64, count four earth beads on the far-right rod (which equals 4). On the next rod to its left, show one heaven bead and one earth bead (50 + 10, or 60). Together, this makes 60 + 4, or 64.

7. Can you show your age on the abacus? How about the year?

A Chinese American weighs medicine at a Chinatown drugstore in San Francisco, about 1890.

4

The 1880s and 1890s

In 1882 prejudice against the Chinese had grown so much that the United States government passed a new law, called the Chinese **Exclusion** Act. It said that no more Chinese laborers could come into the country. Only Chinese merchants, their wives, and a few other groups were allowed in. It took more than forty years for America to end this law.

Because Hawaii was not yet part of the United States, Chinese laborers continued to arrive there in the 1880s and early 1890s. Many worked on **plantations** growing sugar and rice.

Life for the Chinese in America became less safe. In Seattle and some other western cities, Americans forced the Chinese to leave town. Sometimes Americans attacked Chinese businesses or burned their homes.

Yet in spite of danger, discrimination, and hard work, the Chinese found ways to enjoy their culture.

A Chinese opera actress acts out her scene.

Face Painting for Chinese Opera

You are at a Chinese opera with your parents. The show lasts six hours. You and the other few children run back and forth while the actors perform. They wear **brocaded** clothing, fancy hair decorations, and painted faces.

"You can tell what the characters are like from the actors' face paint," your mother explains, when you climb beside her on a bench. "Most of the actors have pink paint around their cheeks and eyes, with white noses and foreheads. But look at that actor over there—he has a big white circle in the middle of his face. That means his character is supposed to be funny."

You will need:

- a partner
- 2 headbands
- washable nontoxic face paints, crayon type, in white, red or pink, and black
- foam cosmetic wedges
- bright red lipstick
- soap, water, sponges, and old towels for cleanup

---

1. Get an adult's permission.

2. Find a partner. Put on headbands to keep your hair away from your faces. Look at the pictures of a hero's face paint (for both male and female characters).

3. With the face paint, color your partner's nose, forehead, chin, and eyebrows white. Add pink or red over the cheeks, blending it in with a cosmetic wedge. Add more pink or red around the eyes, but stay at least ¼ inch away from the eyes themselves.

4. Outline the eyes with black (staying ¼ inch away from the eyes themselves). Draw new eyebrows with black. For fierce characters, draw thick brows that slant down toward your partner's nose and up toward the ear.

5. Put bright red lipstick on your partner's mouth (boy or girl).

6. When done, let your partner paint your face.

7. Take off your headbands, wash your hands, and clean up any mess. Then act out a story.

Girl's Crown

Your family is in a restaurant, celebrating your sister's wedding. Your sister and her new husband are dressed in red. You wear a special crown with beads that hang over your forehead.

Your sister's husband is very lucky, you think. It is hard for Chinese men to find wives, because there aren't many Chinese girls in America. You know it will be easy for your parents to find a good husband for you.

Right now, another dish has been brought to your table—your favorite. You forget about your future and dig in.

Children in traditional Chinese dress.

You will need:

- cloth headband, at least 2 inches wide, in a solid color
- two 7-inch-long pieces of Velcro, both hook and loop sides. Both pieces should be the kind that sticks on without sewing or ironing.
- about 5 feet thin yarn
- scissors
- ruler
- 7-8 beads about ¼ inch across, with large holes

1. Make sure the headband fits.

2. Turn the headband inside out. Lay it down with the seam in back.

3. Attach the loop (fuzzy) strip of Velcro along the top. Be sure the whole piece of Velcro is attached to the cloth. Attach the hook (sharper) piece of Velcro just beneath it.

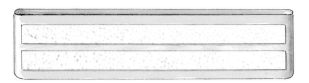

4. Don't touch the Velcro for five minutes. This helps it stick.

5. With the ruler, measure seven to eight pieces of yarn, each about 7 inches long. Then cut them apart. Thread a bead on each. Knot each bead in place with a single knot, in the middle of the piece of yarn.

6. Trim the ends so the distance from each end to the bead is about 3 inches.

7. Lay the pieces of yarn about 1 inch apart on the sharper strip of Velcro. Their ends should come to the top of the sharper part. The bead should dangle about 2 inches below the headband.

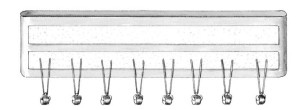

8. Fold the headband so that the two pieces of Velcro come together, with the yarn sandwiched in between.

9. Put the band on your head, either like a crown (if it will stay) or across your forehead, pulling your hair through the back. The beads should dangle around your eyebrows.

Mooncakes

You are a member of a Chinese family living on a sugar plantation in Hawaii. Your father works hard cutting sugar cane while your mother keeps house.

You are helping your mother make mooncakes to sell for tomorrow night's autumn Moon Festival. All the Chinese workers and families will stay up late, eating mooncakes, and saying prayers to Chang O, the Lady of the Moon.

You love mooncakes. These are filled with sweet bean paste and a hard-boiled, salted egg yolk, round as the moon. When your mother turns her back, you raise a cake to your lips.

"Go," says your mother, who couldn't possibly have seen you. "I can finish making these myself."

This recipe uses jam instead of red bean paste and hard-boiled egg yolks instead of special salted ones.

You will need:

- one 18-ounce tube of sugar cookie dough. (You will use about half.)
- 6 hard-boiled eggs, without shells
- strawberry jam
- cutting board
- table knife
- medium-sized bowl
- muffin tin
- 6 paper muffin liners
- ruler
- measuring spoons
- timer or clock
- trivet

1. Ask an adult for help.

2. Preheat the oven to 350 degrees Fahrenheit. Keep the dough refrigerated until step 5.

3. On the cutting board, cut the eggs in half with the knife and remove the egg yolks with your fingers or the knife. Set the yolks aside in the bowl. Discard the whites or use them for something else.

4. Line the six muffin cups with the paper liners.

5. Peel the wrapper from half the cookie dough. Cut seven slices, each about ¼ inch wide. (Look at the ruler.) Discard the end slice. Place the others in the baking cups. Put the dough back in the refrigerator.

6. Press a finger into the middle of each slice to make a dent. Fill each dent with ¼ teaspoon of jam.

7. Center an egg yolk on each slice.

8. With the remaining cookie dough, cut a slice ¼–½ inch wide. With your fingers, carefully pinch it and pull it to make a wider circle of dough. Lay it over one yolk. Repeat this step for the other five mooncakes. Use extra dough to patch any holes. With clean damp fingers, pinch the dough around the edges of each mooncake

9. If the dough gets too sticky, put the muffin tin in the freezer briefly. Wash your hands and try again.

10. Bake about 25 minutes or until medium-brown. Set the hot muffin tin on a trivet to cool.

Glossary

abacus: A wooden frame that holds beads, used for adding, subtracting, multiplying, and dividing.

bachelor: An unmarried man.

bound feet: A fashion in China for centuries. Young girls in wealthier families had their feet wrapped tightly so they would never grow more than three to five inches long. Binding feet became much less common after 1900, when it was banned in China.

brocade: Fancy silk cloth with a raised pattern in silver or gold.

calligraphy: Artistic style of handwriting used by the Chinese.

character: A symbol used in Chinese writing to stand for a word or idea. The Chinese do not use an alphabet to spell words out with letters.

Chinatown: The part of a city or town where most Chinese people lived.

culture: A way of life.

discrimination: Treating people unfairly because of their culture, age, religion, sex, or other features.

exclusion: Keeping people out.

festival: A special celebration, often for a holiday.

immigrant: Someone who moves to another country, planning to stay.

merchant: Someone who buys and sells things for a living.

nineteenth century: The years from 1800 to 1899.

nugget: Tiny chunk.

plantation: A large farm where workers grew crops for the owner to sell.

prejudice: Unfairly seeing some people as not as good as others because of culture, religion, age, sex, or other features.

railroad tie: A wooden beam that supports railroad tracks.

rocker: A simple wooden machine for sifting gold from dirt or sand.

transcontinental: Across the entire continent, from one coast to the other.

Metric Conversion Chart

You can use the chart below to convert from U. S. measurements to the metric system.

Weight
1 ounce = 28 grams
½ pound (8 ounces) = 227 grams
1 pound = .45 kilogram
2.2 pounds = 1 kilogram

Liquid volume
1 teaspoon = 5 milliliters
1 tablespoon = 15 milliliters
1 fluid ounce = 30 milliliters
1 cup = 240 milliliters (.24 liter)
1 pint = 480 milliliters (.48 liter)
1 quart = .95 liter

Length
¼ inch = .6 centimeter
½ inch = 1.27 centimeters
1 inch = 2.54 centimeters

Temperature
100°F = 40°C
110°F = 45°C
350°F = 180°C
375°F = 190°C
400°F = 200°C
425°F = 220°C
450°F = 235°C

Find Out More

Books

Behrens, June. *Gung Hay Fat Choy/Happy New Year.* Chicago: Childrens Press, 1982.

Fraser, Mary Ann. *Ten Mile Day and the Building of the Transcontinental Railroad.* New York: Henry Holt and Company, 1993.

Mayberry, Jodine. *Chinese.* New York: Franklin Watts, 1990.

Russell, Ching Yeung. *Moon Festival.* Honesdale, PA: Boyds Mills Press, 1997.

Raatma, Lucia. *Chinese Americans.* Chanhassen, MN: The Child's World, 2003.

Yep, Laurence. *The Journal of Wong Ming-Chung, A Chinese Miner.* New York: Scholastic, 2000.

Web Sites:

Bay Area Cantonese Opera
www.pearlmagik.com/bayareacantoneseopera/aboutopera.htm

Brief Introduction to the Abacus
www.ee.ryerson.ca:8080/~elf/abacus/intro.html

Central Pacific Railroad Photographic History Museum
www.cprr.org

Chinese New Year
www.educ.uvic.ca/faculty/mroth/438/CHINA/chinese_new_year.html

Harvest Moon Festival
www.educ.uvic.ca/faculty/mroth/438/CHINA/moon.htm

About the Author

Marian Broida has a special interest in hands-on history for children. Growing up near George Washington's home in Mount Vernon, Virginia, Ms. Broida spent much of her childhood pretending she lived in colonial America. She has written six other titles for the Hands-On History series. In addition to children's activity books, she writes books for adults on health care topics and occasionally works as a nurse. Ms. Broida lives in Decatur, Georgia.

Index

DATE DUE